P9-DNG-970

The Bully Blockers Club

Teresa Bateman

ILLUSTRATED BY

Jackie Urbanovic

Albert Whitman & Company, Morton Grove, Illinois

To Jason, Ryan, and Brandon,
who protect the young and small.
And to Sally K.,
who, in every way,
does her best to help them all.—T.B.

For all the teachers in my family: Barb, Tony, Pam,
Jack, Carolyn, Jeannie, Charlie, Joanne, and Michelle;
and teachers everywhere, adults as well as children,
who make a difference.—J.U.

Library of Congress Cataloging-in-Publication Data

Bateman, Teresa.
The Bully Blockers Club/ by Teresa Bateman ; illustrated by Jackie Urbanovic.
p. cm.
Summary: When Lotty is bothered by a bully at school, she helps start a club where everyone is welcome.
ISBN 10: 0-8075-0918-3 (hardcover) ISBN 13: 978-0-8075-0918-0 (hardcover)
ISBN 10: 0-8075-0919-1 (paperback) ISBN 13: 978-0-8075-0919-7 (paperback)
[1. Bullies–Fiction. 2. Clubs–Fiction. 3. Schools–Fiction.] I. Urbanovic, Jackie, ill. II. Title.
PZ7.B294435Bul 2004 [E]–dc22 2004000524

Text copyright © 2004 by Teresa Bateman.
Illustrations copyright © 2004 by Jackie Urbanovic.
Published in 2004 by Albert Whitman & Company, 6340 Oakton Street, Morton Grove, Illinois 60053-2723.
Published simultaneously in Canada by Fitzhenry & Whiteside, Markham, Ontario.
All rights reserved. No part of this book may be reproduced or transmitted in any form or by any means,
electronic or mechanical, including photocopying, recording, or by any information storage and retrieval system,
without permission in writing from the publisher.
Printed in the United States.
10 9 8 7 6 5 4

The design is by Carol Gildar.

For more information about Albert Whitman & Company,
please visit our web site at www.albertwhitman.com.

On Monday, Lotty waved to her mother and skipped to school. She had a new backpack, new shoes, and a new teacher. It was going to be a great year.

But when she sat down at her new desk, someone behind her said, "Yick! What's that smell?"

"What smell?" Lotty asked.

"I'm Grant Grizzly and I say there's a smell, and it's coming from around *you*."

Lotty peered inside her desk and sniffed. Grant Grizzly looked at her, held his nose, and laughed.

Lotty shrank down in her seat. "Maybe I *do* smell," she thought. Her stomach hurt. Her smile slipped.

When Lotty got home, she told her little brother, Jerome, and big sister, Lily, what had happened.

"Should I tell Mrs. Kallberg?" Lotty asked. "I don't want to be a tattletale."

"All Grant did was say something," Jerome pointed out. "If he does it again, give him a karate chop!"

"No karate chops," Lily said, frowning. "And it's not tattling to let the teacher know there's a problem. Still, why don't you try ignoring him first? Maybe he'll leave you alone."

Lotty decided to try Lily's idea.

On Tuesday, she ignored Grant. She ignored the hand that swiped her eraser. She ignored the foot that kicked the back of her chair all morning. She ignored the nasty whispers.

Grant never did anything while the teacher was looking, but he didn't leave Lotty alone. If anything, he got worse.

"She's so stupid she doesn't even know when someone's talking to her," he told his friends in the hall. Then he yelled, "HEY, STUPID!" right in Lotty's face.

Lotty's stomach hurt. Her eyes prickled. She skipped
morning recess and went to the nurse's office, but when the
nurse asked what was wrong, Lotty couldn't say anything.

Later she told Lily and Jerome what had happened.

"Smack him in the nose!" Jerome insisted.

"No nose-smacking!" Lily said. "I think you should tell the teacher."

Lotty shook her head. "What if she thinks I'm a tattletale?"

Lily sighed. "Well then, why don't you try to be his friend? Sometimes kids act that way because they don't have friends."

"Or you could make a joke out of it," Jerome suggested.

Lotty decided to give their ideas a try.

On Wednesday, while Mrs. Kallberg was talking to a parent in the hall, Lotty smiled at Grant. She asked if he liked baseball. She offered to lend him a pencil when he didn't have one.

"I'm allergic to ugly," Grant replied. "And you're giving me a rash."

Lotty tried to laugh. "That's . . . funny," she said.

"I'd rather be funny than funny-looking, Stink-o," Grant replied. Then he knocked all the books off her desk as he went past.

The other kids in the room looked up at the noise. Then they saw Grant and looked quickly down again.

Lotty's stomach hurt, her eyes prickled, and her shoulders drooped.

That night Lotty picked at her dinner.

"What's wrong?" her father asked.

"You're awfully quiet," her mother said.

Lotty tried to smile, but she burst into tears.

Lily and Jerome explained everything that had happened.

"Why didn't you tell us before?" her mother asked.

"Why didn't you tell Mrs. Kallberg?"

"Tomorrow morning I'm calling your teacher," her father said. "If Grant bothers you again, look him in the eye and tell him to stop. Keep telling him until he does, and make sure that Mrs. Kallberg knows."

Thursday morning, Mrs. Kallberg called Lotty and Grant to her desk.

"Is there a problem?" she asked.

"No problem here," Grant said, smiling.

Lotty was afraid to say anything, with Grant standing right there.

The teacher waited, and finally said, "Everyone at our school is supposed to feel safe. If you don't feel safe, you need to tell an adult. That's not tattling. If you're making other people feel unsafe, then you are breaking a school rule. Understand?"

She looked at Grant and Lotty.

"I got it," Grant said, and headed back to his desk.

Lotty nodded silently. Mrs. Kallberg leaned forward. "I'll keep an eye out," she said. "So will the other adults."

Lotty nodded again, but she wasn't sure it was going to help.

At lunch, after checking to make sure no adults were watching, Grant swiped Lotty's dessert.

"You're so fat you don't need cake," he said, stuffing it in his own mouth.

Lotty's knees rattled and her throat was dry, but she remembered her father's advice. She looked into Grant's face and said, "I don't like what you're doing. Leave me alone."

Grant laughed and grabbed her sandwich
and grapes. "How're you gonna stop me?"
he asked and walked away.

Lotty wasn't hungry anymore anyway.

When she told her family what Grant had done, they were upset.

"You're not fat," her mother said.

"You actually look sort of OK," Jerome added. "I mean, for a girl."

"I'll leave your teacher a message again tonight," her father said, "and I'll stop by and see her tomorrow after school. Did you tell her about this?"

Jerome rolled his eyes. "What are *teachers* going to do?" he asked. "They can't follow her around all day."

Lotty thought about what Jerome had said. It was true that Grant usually left her alone when grownups were watching. But grownups weren't always around. Who was?

Suddenly she smiled. "Please don't call or go to school yet," she told her father. "Give me a chance to try something first."

Friday morning, Lotty watched Grant
push Laurie down. She watched him swipe
Barney's homework. She watched him cut
in line and knock Ben's books out of his
hands. She noticed Grant only acted
that way when grownups
weren't looking.

After lunch, Lotty found Laurie and Barney and Ben.
"I saw what Grant did to you today, and I have an idea,"
she said. "Let's form a club."
She explained her plan.

That afternoon, when Grant grabbed
Lotty's crayons, Barney said, "Hey, what
are you doing?"

"Yeah," said Laurie. "Those aren't yours."

By now everyone, including Mrs. Kallberg,
was watching.

Grant turned red, and handed the crayons back.

At afternoon recess, when Grant
grabbed Barney's soccer ball, Ben,
Lotty, and Laurie were there. They
didn't yell. They just asked, loudly,
what he thought he was doing.

The playground supervisor
came over to see what they were
talking about.

Grant gave the ball back.

"What business is it of yours?"
he asked the friends.

"It's club business," they replied.

On Monday morning, school began a little differently. Mrs. Kallberg told the class they were skipping math that day. "There have been some problems at school, so today every class is talking about bullying, safety, and making everyone feel welcome.

"How do you feel when someone's bullying you?" she asked.

"Sad," said Laurie.

"Scared," Lotty whispered.

"Sick," Barney added.

"Lonely," "Angry," other children said.

Grant was silent.

On the chalkboard:

Friends
e welcoming
hare
e kind
et others play

Bullies
Ignore them
Walk away
Tell them to stop
~~Fight back~~
Tell a grownup

"Could we come up with some rules so that people don't have to feel sad, scared, sick, lonely, or angry?" Mrs. Kallberg asked.

There was a pause. Then hands flew up. Mrs. Kallberg wrote suggestions on the board.

Then Lotty told everyone about the club.

Over the next few days, other kids at school heard about the club. "Can we join, too?" they asked.

"Sure," Lotty and her friends replied. "Everyone's welcome." Barney even came up with a great name for their club—"The Bully Blockers."

"Almost everybody's a member now," Lotty reported. "It's nice keeping an eye out for other people."

Things got better after that. Kids spoke up when they saw something wrong and reached out to anyone who looked lonely.

"Hey, you want to play, too?"

"*Me?*"

"Sure!"

The adults were watching, too, at lunchtime and at recess and in the halls.

After a while, Grant didn't seem as big and scary. One morning he even helped Lotty when her backpack spilled.

"Here's your lunch," he said.

Lotty smiled. "Thanks."

A few days later, Lotty skipped to school. She had new friends, a new attitude, and a new club. It was going to be a great year.

The Bully Blockers was a brilliant idea.

She wasn't about to tell Jerome that he'd given it to her.

About Bullying

Getting along with others is an important skill that all children must acquire. Sometimes conflicts occur, and learning how to resolve these conflicts peacefully is vital. Teasing is unacceptable, and makes children feel uncomfortable. Bullying, however, is more than this. Bullies assume power over their victims, making other children feel scared, unsafe, or helpless. This behavior happens repeatedly.

Whether physical or verbal, bullying hurts, and immediate action must be taken. Adults and children need to learn how to evaluate a situation, choose the safest course of action, and determine when a problem can be solved by the child and when adult intervention is necessary.

Often children hesitate to report bullying. They're afraid of what the bully might do, concerned that they might not be believed, and aware of the stigma of "tattling." Adults must make it clear that it's right to report a threatening situation, whether it happened to the child personally or was something he or she witnessed.

When a child is bullied, we encourage him or her to try to befriend the bully. If that isn't possible, the child might use the TELL IT system:

Think before you react.

Express yourself. Clearly state how you feel.

Leave the situation. Walk away.

Laugh it off. Use humor to defuse the situation.

Ignore the bully.

Tell a trusted adult.

When children practice all these skills by role-playing, they learn how to cope in real life.

Creating supportive groups is another way to stop bullying. Bullies often target children who are alone or different. When all children are part of a caring, involved community, there is less opportunity for bullying and more room for growth and friendship.

Ultimately, the key is awareness. Children and adults need to be aware of what is going on around them. Unacceptable behavior must be reported and dealt with immediately. Action must be taken whenever any child feels threatened. Working together, we can create an environment where all children feel safe and accepted.